MW00896721

To my sweet family: Krystian, Ania and Adam
-Tianna

For mom
-Nat

Two Blondies Press

Text Copyright © 2020 Tianna Gawlak
Illustrations Copyright © 2020 Natalie Lundeen
All rights reserved, including the right of
reproduction in whole or in part in any form.
ISBN 978-0-578-70269-8

www.twoblondiespress.com

When You Dream of Chocolate Cake

Tianna Gawlak

illustrated by Natalie Lundeen

When my mom tucked me in tonight, she told me with a smile,
"Hurry off to sleep so that you can dream a while."

Before she left the bedroom, I noticed on her sleeve
A splotch of something brown and light- cocoa, I believe.

I know because mom and I bake together often.
She likes to give me baking tips, like butter should be softened.

I think of all these memories, and then I close my eyes.
What I tell you next should really come as no surprise.

I dreamt of creamy chocolate, layered in a cake,
and endless rows of sweet treats right there for me to take.

Cheesecakes and apple pies- oh my, did they look dreamy!
Fresh from the oven, too, I could see they were still steamy.

The cream puffs were so stuffed, and the fruit tarts were just right.
The macarons with buttercream were really quite a sight.

I walked the rows and rubbed my eyes, could this really be?
All these rich and splendid treats, who made them all for me?

Of all the treats before me, one really caught my eye.
Chocolate cake with creamy layers, I couldn't pass on by.

I turned and made a run for it, I wanted to take a bite.
But as I moved in closer, it vanished from my sight!

Impossible, this can't be! Wasn't it just here?
I turned around to search for it, hoping it was near.

Crawling on my hands and knees, I searched across the floor.
I'd been rummaging a while, I thought, "Just a minute more."

Suddenly, I heard a loud beeping in the distance.
Could it be a timer? The ringing had persistence.

That's when I got a whiff of something freshly baked.
Rich cake and luscious cream, my sweet tooth really ached.

beep beep beep beep beep beep beep

The chocolate cake with creamy layers sat there on the plate.
When that first bite touched my lips, it felt like it was fate.

Then I had to ask her, "How did you know my dream?
Why did you bake this chocolate cake with perfect buttercream?"

She said, "You have five senses, that work hard to explain
What you see, smell, hear, taste, touch, and then they tell your brain."

see

smell

taste

hear

touch

I paused to think about it, had my senses played a role?
Did they know my mom was baking? Had they been in control?

I'd seen the cocoa on mom's sleeve

and smelled the lovely cream.

I'd heard the timer ringing,

knew the cake would taste supreme.

While it started to make sense now, that didn't answer why,
Why bake cake to begin? I waited for her reply.

"Sweet treats make me feel good. Their taste is a delight.
I like to share sweet things with you, so I made this cake at night.

My days are long and busy. There's so much for me to do.
But even when I'm busy, I always think of you.

May this cake be your reminder, awake or when asleep
That as your mom I love you always, my love for you runs deep."

I took the fork and with a smile I split the cake in two.
Half for her and half for me, "Mommy, I love you too!"

Can you find these objects?

whisk   bowl   timer   pan   apron   spatula   mixer   fork   glass of milk

Chocolate Cake
Recipe by Natasha's Kitchen

Ingredients for Chocolate Cake:

3 cups all-purpose flour
1/2 cup unsweetened cocoa powder (natural)
2 cups granulated sugar
2 tsp baking soda
1 tsp salt
2 cups warm coffee (not hot)
2 Tbsp white vinegar
1 Tbsp vanilla extract
2/3 cup light olive oil not extra virgin

Ingredients for Chocolate Frosting:

12 oz cream cheese room temperature
1 cup unsalted butter (16 Tbsp) room temperature
5 cups powdered sugar
1 cup unsweetened cocoa powder (natural)
1/2 tsp salt
2 tsp vanilla extract

Making the Cake Layers:

1. Preheat the oven to 350°F. Butter two 9" cake pans and line the bottoms with a ring of parchment paper.
2. In a large bowl whisk together your dry ingredients: 3 cups flour, 1/2 cup cocoa powder, 2 cups sugar, 2 tsp baking soda and 1 tsp salt until there are no more cocoa lumps (a few tiny lumps are ok; it also helps to sift the cocoa before using it).
3. In a separate bowl, mix together your wet ingredients: 2 cups warm coffee, 2 Tbsp vinegar, 1 Tbsp vanilla extract and 2/3 cup olive oil.

4. Whisk the wet ingredients into the dry ingredients just until they come together. Your batter will still be slightly lumpy. Divide equally between prepared cake pans, and bake in a preheated oven at 350°F for 35 minutes or until a toothpick comes out clean. Let cool in the pan 15 minutes then transfer to a wire rack to cool completely before frosting.

Making the Chocolate Frosting:

1. In the bowl of an electric mixer using paddle attachment (or using an electric hand mixer with a large bowl), beat together 12 oz cream cheese with 1 cup butter on medium/high speed until creamy (3 min), scraping down the bowl as needed.
2. Sift in 5 cups powdered sugar with 1 cup cocoa powder, sifting in batches as needed to ensure there are no lumps. Then add 1/2 tsp salt. Mix on low speed until well combined. Thoroughly scrape down the bowl, then increase to medium/high speed and beat until smooth and whipped (1 min).
3. Add 2 tsp vanilla and beat on medium/high until smooth (1 min). Now it's ready to be piped onto cooled cake.

www.natashaskitchen.com

Recipe and Photographs Copyright © 2020 Natasha's Kitchen

CPSIA information can be obtained
at www.ICGtesting.com
Printed in the USA
LVHW070428130721
692524LV00005B/42

9 780578 726250